THE MIGHTY THOR

This Is
THE MIGHTY THOR

Adapted by **Emeli Juhlin**

Illustrated by **Devin Taylor** *and* **Vita Efemova**

Based on the Marvel comic book character **The Mighty Thor**

MARVEL

Los Angeles
New York

© 2022 MARVEL

For information address Marvel Press, 77 West 66th Street, New York, New York, 10023.

Printed in the United States of America
First Edition, March 2022   10 9 8 7 6 5 4 3 2 1
Library of Congress Control Number: 2021931838
FAC-029261-22014
ISBN: 978-1-368-07021-8

This is Jane Foster.

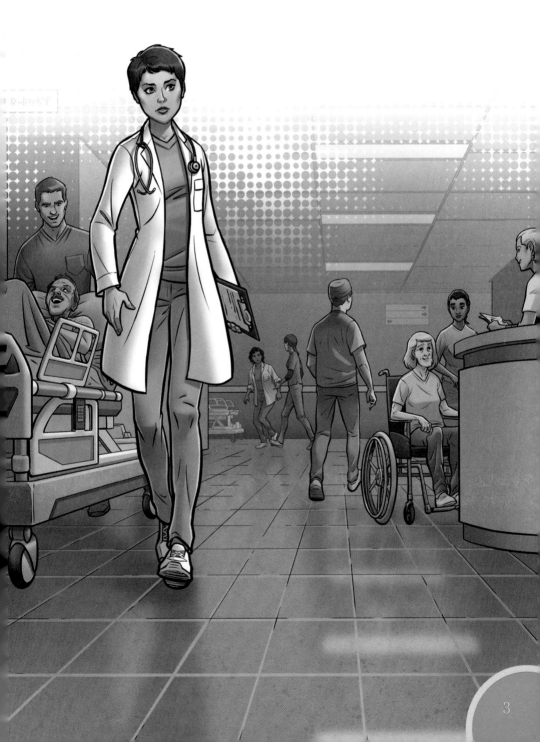

Jane is a doctor.
She helps people.

Jane is sick.

Thor is worried about her.

Jane meets the Avengers.

They also help people.

Thor cannot lift his hammer.

He must fight without it.

Thor's hammer calls to Jane.

She can lift the hammer.

Whosoever holds this hammer, if they be worthy, shall possess the power of . . . **Thor**

The hammer changes Jane.
She becomes The Mighty Thor!

It is what she is meant to do.

Jane is not sick when
she uses the hammer.

The Mighty Thor is very brave.
She uses her powers for good.

She saves lives.
That is important to her.

Black Widow needs her help.

The Mighty Thor flies fast.

Black Widow caught a thief.

It is Loki!

He fights the
super heroes.

Loki cannot win.

Black Widow and
The Mighty Thor stop him.

The police thank them.

The super heroes saved the day!

The Mighty Thor teams up
with the Avengers.

It is her job to protect people.
It is what she is meant to do.

Jane is The Mighty Thor!